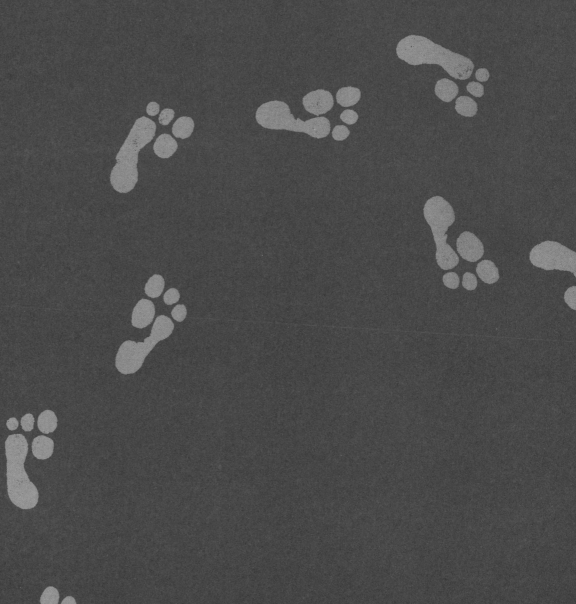

Written by **Lisa Wheeler**   Illustrated by **Chris Van Dusen**

Even MONSTERS Need to SLEEP

BALZER + BRAY
An Imprint of HarperCollins*Publishers*

Balzer + Bray is an imprint of HarperCollins Publishers.

Even Monsters Need to Sleep
Text copyright © 2017 by Lisa Wheeler
Illustrations copyright © 2017 by Chris Van Dusen

information address HarperCollins Children's Books, a division of HarperCollins
Publishers, 195 Broadway, New York, NY 10007.
www.harpercollinschildrens.com

ISBN 978-0-06-236640-5

The illustrations were done in gouache.
16 17 18 19 20   SCP   10 9 8 7 6 5 4 3 2 1
❖ First Edition
Typography by Dana Fritts

HEE
HEE

For Sylvie, who has a world of books ahead of her.
—L.W.

In memory of my best friend, Dave—
the most lovable monster I ever knew.
—C.V.D.

When Bigfoot goes to bed each night,

he hugs his wooby extra tight

and leaves on just a little light.

Even Bigfoot needs to sleep.

Aliens in UFOs
wear fuzzy-wuzzy bedtime clothes.
They pillow-fight until they doze.
Even aliens need to sleep.

Dragon dozes in a nest—
between her mom and dad is best.
She talks and talks . . . then *finally* rests.
Even dragons need to sleep.

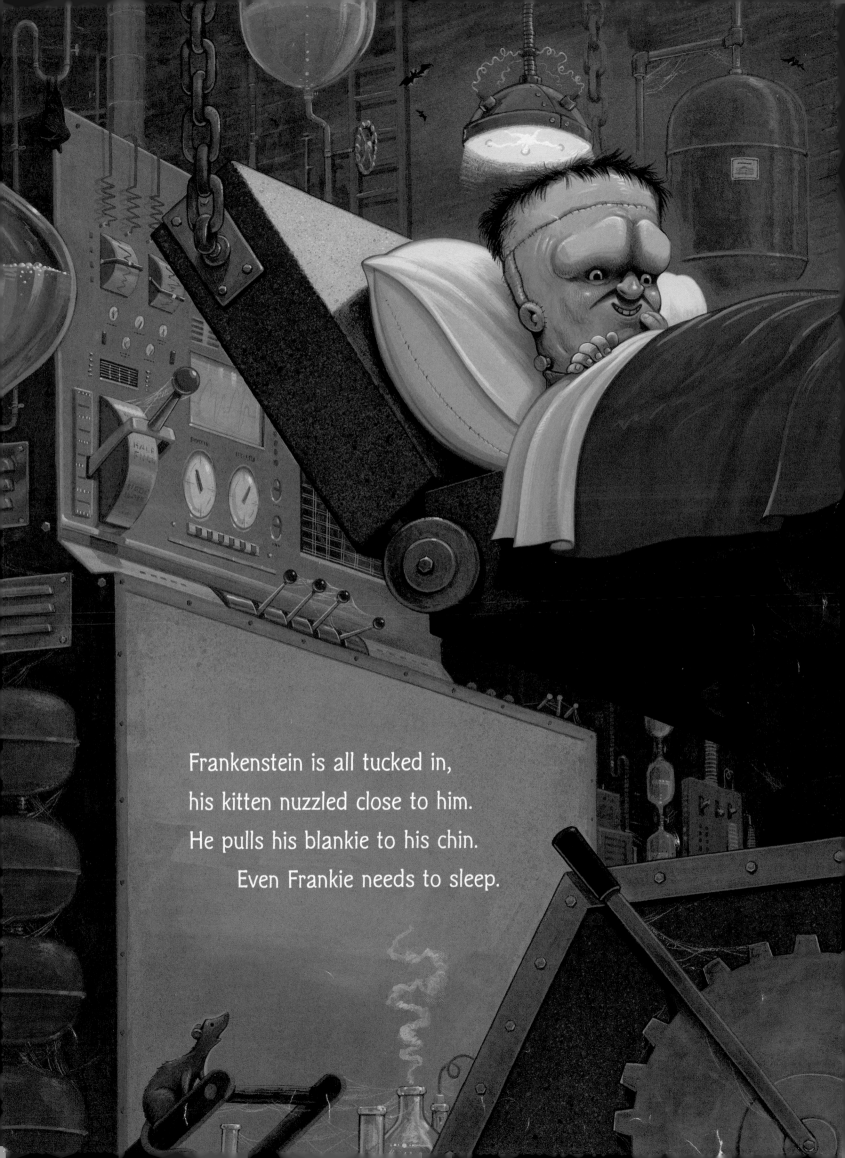

Frankenstein is all tucked in,
his kitten nuzzled close to him.
He pulls his blankie to his chin.
Even Frankie needs to sleep.

Yeti puts away his sled,
then trudges to his snowy bed.

He makes a snack . . .

then rests his head.
Even Yeti needs to sleep.

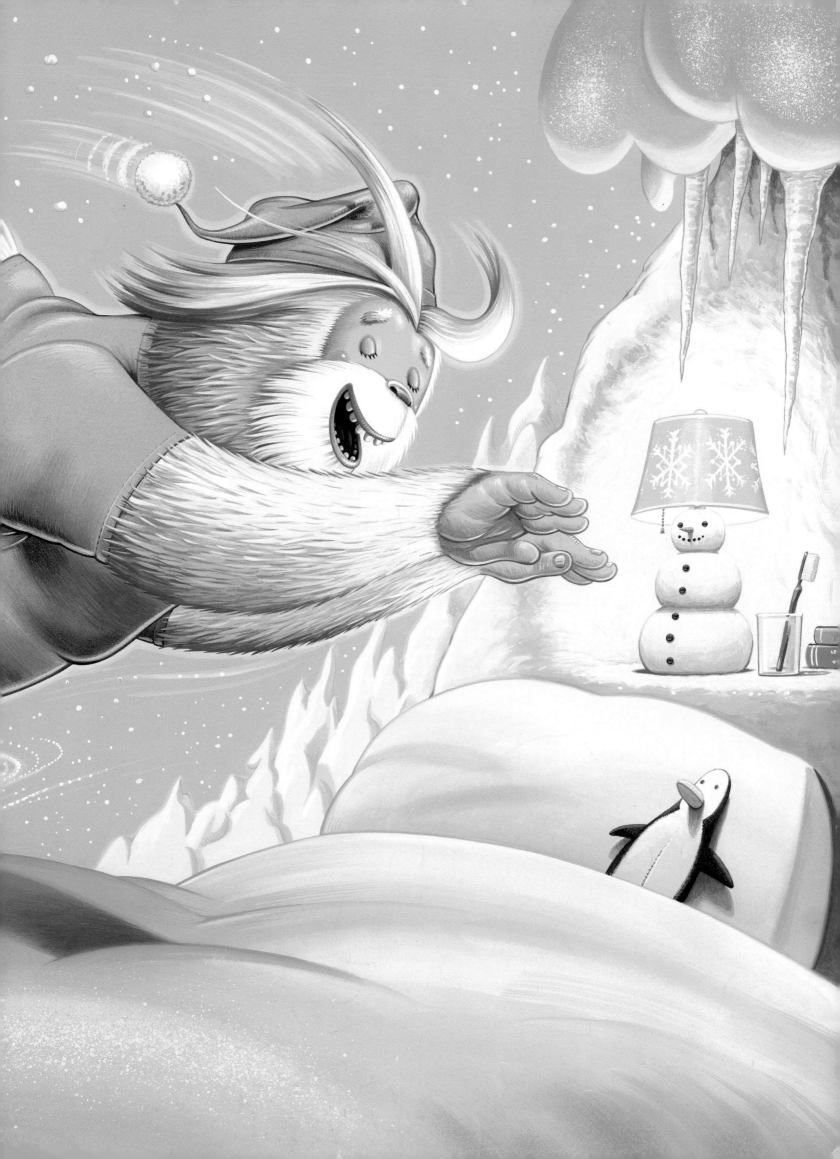

Troll's big-boy bed is by a brook,

tucked inside a comfy nook.

Nanny reads his favorite book.

Even bridge trolls need to sleep.

When Loch Ness Monster needs to sleep,
she gets a drink . . .
         then gets a drink . . .
              then gets a drink . . .
then swims down deep
to kelp beds where she's counting sheep.
         Even Nessie needs to sleep.

When Giant's tired he whines and cries,

then finds a bed to fit his size.

He sucks his thumb and shuts his eyes.
Even giants need to sleep.

Monsters have a bedtime, too.
Their dad sings them a song or two,
then checks beneath the bed for YOU!
Even monsters need to sleep.

So close your eyes and have no fear.
You're safe and sound with loved ones near.
Hush for now. Don't make a peep!
All little monsters need to sleep.

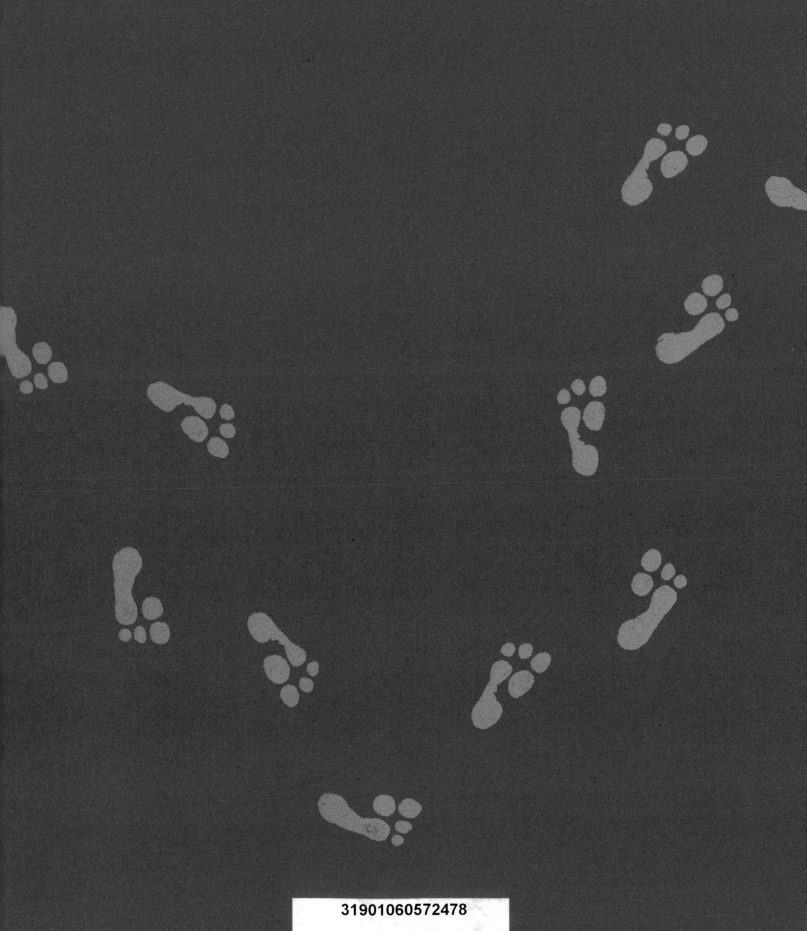